In
1935 if you wanted to
read a good book, you needed
either a lot of money or a library card.
Cheap paperbacks were available, but their
poor production generally mirrored the quality
between the covers. One weekend that year,
Allen Lane, Managing Director of The Bodley Head,
having spent the weekend visiting Agatha Christie,
found himself on a platform at Exeter station trying to
find something to read for his journey back to London.
He was appalled by the quality of the material he had to
choose from. Everything that Allen Lane achieved from that
day until his death in 1970 was based on a passionate belief
in the existence of 'a vast reading public for *intelligent*
books at a low price'. The result of his momentous vision
was the birth not only of Penguin, but of the 'paperback
revolution'. Quality writing became available for the price of
a packet of cigarettes, literature became a mass medium
for the first time, a nation of book-borrowers became a
nation of book-buyers – and the very concept of book
publishing was changed for ever. Those founding
principles – of quality and value, with an overarching
belief in the fundamental importance of reading –
have guided everything the company has
done since 1935. Sir Allen Lane's
pioneering spirit is still very much alive
at Penguin in 2005. Here's to
the next 70 years!

MORE THAN A BUSINESS

'We decided it was time to end the almost customary half-hearted manner in which cheap editions were produced – as though the only people who could possibly want cheap editions must belong to a lower order of intelligence. We, however, believed in the existence in this country of a vast reading public for intelligent books at a low price, and staked everything on it'
Sir Allen Lane, 1902–1970

'The Penguin Books are splendid value for sixpence, so splendid that if other publishers had any sense they would combine against them and suppress them'
George Orwell

'More than a business … a national cultural asset'
Guardian

'When you look at the whole Penguin achievement you know that it constitutes, in action, one of the more democratic successes of our recent social history'
Richard Hoggart

Design Faults in the Volvo 760 Turbo

WILL SELF

PENGUIN BOOKS

PENGUIN BOOKS

Published by the Penguin Group
Penguin Books Ltd, 80 Strand, London WC2R ORL, England
Penguin Group (USA) Inc., 375 Hudson Street, New York, New York 10014, USA
Penguin Group (Canada), 10 Alcorn Avenue, Toronto, Ontario, Canada M4V 3B2
(a division of Pearson Penguin Canada Inc.)
Penguin Ireland, 25 St Stephen's Green, Dublin 2, Ireland
(a division of Penguin Books Ltd)
Penguin Group (Australia), 250 Camberwell Road, Camberwell, Victoria 3124,
Australia (a division of Pearson Australia Group Pty Ltd)
Penguin Books India Pvt Ltd, 11 Community Centre,
Panchsheel Park, New Delhi – 110 017, India
Penguin Group (NZ), cnr Airborne and Rosedale Roads, Albany,
Auckland 1310, New Zealand (a division of Pearson New Zealand Ltd)
Penguin Books (South Africa) (Pty) Ltd, 24 Sturdee Avenue,
Rosebank 2196, South Africa

Penguin Books Ltd, Registered Offices: 80 Strand, London WC2R ORL, England

www.penguin.com

Tough, Tough Toys for Tough, Tough Boys first published by Bloomsbury 1998
Reprinted by kind permission of Grove/Atlantic, Inc., USA
This selection published as a Pocket Penguin 2005

1

Set in 11/13pt Monotype Dante
Typeset by Palimpsest Book Production Limited
Polmont, Stirlingshire
Printed in England by Clays Ltd, St Ives plc

Contents

Design Faults in the
Volvo 760 Turbo: A Manual

'. . . bearing in mind the fact that everyone hides
the truth in matters of sex . . .'

– Sigmund Freud,
'My Views on the Part Played by Sexuality
in the Aetiology of the Neuroses'

1. Instruments and Controls

Welcome to the terrifyingly tiny world of the urban
adulterer. Bill Bywater has been snogging with a
woman called Serena. Giving and receiving as much
tongue as possible – exactly at the point where Sussex
Gardens terminate, and the streams of traffic whip
around the dusty triangular enclosure of trees and
grass, before peeling away in the direction of Hyde
Park, or Paddington, or the M40.

Bill has been snogging – and the adolescent term
is quite appropriate here – in a way he remembers
from youth. Not that the palpings of lip-on-lip,
tongue-on-lip, and tongue-on-tongue have been any
less accomplished, or plosively erotic, than we have

come to expect from the man. It's just that Serena has recently had an operation on a benign cyst in her cheek. Bit of Lidocaine. Slit and suck – two stitches. Bosh-bosh. 'Perhaps it would be wise' – the surgeon had said, admiring the creamy skin of her cleavage, the standing into being of her ever-so-slightly large breasts – 'if you were to avoid using your mouth for anything much besides eating over the next week or so?'

He was right to make this statement interrogative – almost verging on the rhetorical, because Serena hardly uses her mouth for eating at all, preferring dietary supplements and cocaine to get by on. Serena used to be an 'it' girl – but now she's 'that' woman. A socialite – she went to a finishing school in Switzerland where they taught her to fellate. She'd set her cap at Bill months ago. Not that he wasn't ripe for it.

Serena says, 'I've had a small operation on my cheek . . .' The eyelashes perturb the polluted air, monoxide and burnt rubber. 'Try and be gentle with this side –' She caresses her own elastoplasted cheek. Their bodies marry. Her thighs part slightly to receive the buttressing of his thigh. Her lips begin to worry at his mouth – so adept Bill wonders if they might be prehensile. He allows his hands to link in the region of her coccyx. A thumb lazily traces the rivulets and curves between her arse and the small of her back. She moans into his mouth. The traffic groans into his ear. He concentrates on stimulating the side of her which isn't numb.

As he is snogging, Bill is acutely aware of the time: 6.30 p.m.; the place: Sussex Gardens, W2; and the implied logistics: his wife, Vanessa, cycles home every evening along Sussex Gardens, at more or less this time. It is not unlikely that Vanessa will see Bill snogging with Serena, because Bill is – he acknowledges with a spurt of dread – at least sixty feet high. He bestrides the two lanes of bumpy tarmac, his crotch forming a blue denim underpass for the rumbling traffic. Vanessa will be able to see him – this Colossus of Roads – the very instant she jolts across the intersection of the Edgware Road, and commences pedalling down Sussex Gardens.

Caught bang to rights, caught snogging with this slapper . . . His only defence, the fact that she's a little dolly of a thing compared to him. He's holding her aloft in one hand, clutching her wiggling torso to his huge, bristly cheek. He's having to be so damn gentle, tasting with his forty-inch tongue the sweetness of her two-inch bud. Her white satin shift dress has ridden up over her hips. She isn't wearing any tights – her pants are white, with an embroidered panel over her pubis.

'Bill!' Vanessa shouts up from below – she's ramming her front tyre against his foot, the knobble of uncomfortable bone protruding above the edge of his moccasins. 'Bill – what are you doing!?'

'Doing?' He squints down at her, as if she's caught him in an inconsequential reverie – stagnantly considering the cost-effectiveness of double glazing, or fully

3

comprehensive insurance. 'Doing?' He looks at the writhing, half-stripped woman in his hand, and then sets her down, gingerly, on the far side of the road from his wife. 'Oh *her*, or rather – *this*. It's just a doll, my love – you can't possibly be jealous of a *doll*.'

Couldn't be jealous of a doll, but might well be jealous of Serena who is not only a doll, but who has also, predictably, been a model. Bill, feeling the laser beams of his wife's gaze burning through buildings, fences, filing cabinets, people, had broken the embrace – which was getting nowhere. Or rather, it was getting somewhere only too fast. What could he do with Serena, short of hiring a room in the Lancaster Hotel for half an hour? No, that would show up on his credit card statement. They were too old for Hyde Park bushes, and the Volvo 760 Turbo was out of the question on account of various design faults.

Serena had been having a session with her therapist, who had his consulting rooms on Sussex Gardens. Bill had arranged to meet her by her car. A metal rendezvous. Serena had a Westminster permit – Bill didn't. He couldn't find a meter for aeons – he imagined her growing old, her face wizening, an old apple on a draining board. When he did eventually find a space – by the needle exchange Portakabin on South Wharf Road – he had neither pound coins nor twenty-pence pieces. He wanted to ejaculate and die – simultaneously. He stopped one, two, three passers-by – got enough to pay for twenty minutes' snogging. Park up

4

the Volvo – and grab a vulva. Pay for space – space to live.

The minutes tick away in her wounded mouth. Until – confident that at any minute he'll get a ticket – Bill breaks from Serena. 'Call!' they call to each other as he staggers back across the road and disappears in the direction of Paddington Station.

Not that he's out of danger yet. Bill starts up the Volvo and savours its clicking, ticking and peeping into life. But when he pulls away he realises – given that he has absolutely no justification for being in this part of London, on this day, at this time – that the car is grotesquely elongated. When he turns right out of London Street and on to Sussex Gardens, the back end of the vehicle is still in Praed Street. When he reaches the lights on the corner of Westbourne Street, his tail end is still blocking the last set of lights, causing traffic in all four directions to back up, and engendering a healthy tirade of horn-accompanied imprecations: 'Youuuu fuuuucking waaaanker!'

Deciding that the only way he can escape detection – given that he's driving an eighty-foot-long vehicle – is to head for the Westway flyover, Bill turns right. As he circles the triangular enclosure where he snogged with Serena, he is appalled to see that the back end of the Volvo is passing by on the other side. He looks through the rear windows of his own car and can see sweet wrappers and medical journals scattered around on the back seat. Jesus! Astonishing how ductile these Volvo chassis are – they know what they're about over there at the Kalmar Plant. Know what they're about when it comes to building an eighty-foot extrudomobile like this, that can be seen clearly from a mile away . . .

Bill Bywater, feeling the Volvo concertina back to its normal length, as he gains the anonymity of the motorway flyover, scrabbles in the breast pocket of his shirt for a cigarette. He lights it with a disposable gas lighter. The dash lighter has long since gone. Bill airily lit a fag with it a year or so ago, waved it gently in the air, and then threw it out the car window. One of the design faults – although hardly limited to the Volvo 760 Turbo – was this lack of a tether.

Another was the ashtray itself. This was accommodated neatly enough, in the central housing of the dash, but it was impossible to pull the tray out at all unless the shift was in drive; and fully out only if it was in first gear. The implications of this stagger Bill anew as he struggles to insinuate his ash-tipped fag into the small gap. Could it be that the car *cognoscenti* at Kalmar intended this as an anti-smoking measure? It hardly made sense. For the ashtray couldn't be opened at all when the shift was in park – implying that you should only smoke, and even empty the ashtray, when the car was in motion.

The Volvo is passing Ladbroke Grove tube station, doing around seventy. Bill can see commuters tramping the platform. And anyway – even if the operation was technically difficult – he did at least know how to empty the ashtray. The manual expressed it quite succinctly: 'Empty ashtrays by pulling out to the limit and pressing down the tongue.'

Bill was masterful at this – he could even avoid the cyst.

2. Body and Interior

Bill has arranged to meet Serena at a pub in Maida Vale. It's a barn of a gaff on Cunningham Place – so prosaic it might even be called The Cunningham. It's the night of a vital World Cup qualifier for England, and the city soup is being insistently thickened by cars, as the spectators head for their home terraces. The driving is stop-start – and so is the parking. Eventually, he finds a tight space on Hamilton Terrace. He cuts in well enough the first time, but the space is so confined that he has to turn the steering wheel in the other direction, then back, then reverse again, each time gaining just a few inches more of the precious, temporary possession.

With each rotation the power steering 'Eeeeee-youuuus' – a fluid, pleasurable kind of whine; and with each dab on brake, or plunge on accelerator, the rubber limbs buck, receiving pressure or its release. 'In-Glands! In-Glands! In-Glands!' his pulse chants in his temples. Bill feels exposed – in this act of taking the space; worries that he may be observed, censured. When he's finally got himself and the car properly berthed – no more than six inches to front and aft –

he lunges out the door, giddy in the hot, sappy, fume-tangy evening air. But there's nothing; only an old woman with secateurs in a front garden; the roar of traffic from the Edgware Road; a Tourettic man – gnome-like with a spade of grey beard – who high-steps it over the domed camber of the road, legs smiting his chest, whilst he expels a series of sharp 'Papp-papp-papp!' sounds.

Bill is reassured. In a London uncaring enough to ignore such blatancy – the Tourettic looking as if he were on a run-up to jumping clear of his own nervous system – Bill's own peccadilloes *not even consummated, as yet*, can hardly be of any interest at all. Still, it takes him five minutes of walking up the road, patting his pockets, retracing his steps to see if he has forgotten anything, or dropped anything, or illegally parked the car – only too easy to do in a city where the controls of adjoining zones are radically different – before he resigns himself to the concrete reality of the rendezvous. He is going to meet Serena – this time he might fuck her.

Serena is sitting on one of the four trestle-table-and-bench combinations that occupy the dirty oblong of paving in between The Cunningham itself, and the low brick wall that borders it. A very believable terrace – for London. There are metal ashtrays with beer spilt into them, there are crisp packets wedged in the tabletop cracks, there are sunshades poking through two of these tabletops. One advertises Martini – the other is in tatters. The compression of boozing bodies within the cavernous boozer is already considerable; the baying of the clientele and the baying of the Wembley crowd – relayed by a giant-screen television suspended from the ceiling – are echoing one another. The beery exhalations surge from the double doors of the pub; which are propped back, so as to allow the T-shirted multi-lung to draw in another great gulp of exhausted air.

Bill considers that this rendezvous is taking place within a spatial gap – the Edgware Road/Maida Vale hinterland – and, more importantly, a temporal one. 'I can't stand all this nationalist sporting triumphalism' – he has been priming Vanessa the five days since he avoided Serena's cyst – 'it's going to reach a hideous climax . . . And then what – when they lose there'll be a national depression for days. I can't stand it. I want to opt out.'

Of course, what Bill really wants to opt out of is any situation of *bonhomie*, of excitation, that might embrace them – and tighten up the vice of fidelity. Bill has been working on his dissatisfactions with Vanessa for weeks now – building up a comprehensive dossier of her awfulness. Without this adulterers' manifesto Bill knows he'll be incapable of being remotely serene – with Serena. It would only take one embrace, one shared apprehension, for him to have to abandon his plans. Therefore, why not excise this possibility *and* use the time available.

'Shit! It's all shit!' he had cried an hour or so before. 'I can't stand it – I'm off out. I've got to find somewhere – anywhere where nobody's concerned about this fucking football match!' He then grabbed his car keys from the hall table, performed an uninteresting arabesque in the process of snatching up the CD face-off and his mobile phone, before slamming the door and sprinting off up the garden path. Vanessa, who was sat marking spelling tests, wondered what the hell her husband was on about – she wasn't remotely interested in the football international; and their two-year-old son was, somewhat proleptically, already at his grandmother's.

'Hi!' says Serena – who cares nothing for Bill's predicament, who indeed positively savours it. 'I thought you wouldn't make it.'

'Traffic – parking.' He fobs her off with his key fob. 'Have you got a drink?' She downs the rest of her sea breeze and downs the glass.

'No.'

He shuttles in and out of the bar over the next half-hour. Serena has four more sea breezes – a nicely paradoxical drink for this landlocked Saragossa. Bill struggles to keep his alcohol intake down; tonight has undoubtedly seen the inception of a special Metropolitan Police Task Force to deal with adulterous drunk drivers. Every time he thinks she isn't looking – he checks his watch. The seconds are ticking by towards half-time. In the meantime they edge closer as well.

Serena is wearing a black suede miniskirt. It has six brass buttons to fasten it at the front – but the three bottom ones are undone. Serena is wearing a cream silk blouse and no bra. Serena never wears tights in summer – her legs are too good. Each time she leans forward Bill sucks her nipples; each time she leans back he runs his bent-back index finger up the front of her pants. Not.

Bill dives into the public bar of The Cunningham and edges through the crowd of passive dribblers. 'Awwwww!' they cry – awed by some feat of failure. It takes several such 'awws' and accompanying pokes in the ribs for Bill to gain the far side of the public bar, and the stairs down to the toilets. In the toilet he releases the trap of his flies and the grey hound of penis comes out frothing. Painful – peeing with an erection – Bill has to force himself into alarming postures in order to lend his urine to the giant ceramic ear. While he's doing this he reflects on the paradoxical sense of control offered by reckless driving.

That's what he needs – to get Serena away from the pub, get her in the Volvo, take her for a spin. There's a vanity mirror set into the passenger-seat sunshade – she'll like that. And there'll be no chance of being observed by anyone who knows either of them – or Bill's wife. Even if Bill's wife were to suddenly manifest herself in the Volvo – Serena could hide in the glove compartment, as any other adulterer might hide in a cupboard. She really was a doll.

3. Starting and Driving

It takes the same brake shoe-shuffle to extract the Volvo (overall length four metres and seventy-nine centimetres) from the parking space. Bill, as he circles the steering wheel back and forth, wishes he were coming rather than going – because he could then make some crack to Serena, analogise the parking space and *her* space.

They pop up on to the crown of Hamilton Terrace and Bill turns the big car to the north. He is conscious of Serena on the seat beside him, her thighs slightly parted, her trunk slightly tilted in his direction, a tip of pink tongue between her scarlet lips. 'How's the cyst?' he forays – they have yet to snog.

'Better!' she laughs, a horrible, expensive, phone-your-divorce-lawyer kind of laugh. She is – Bill reflects – an awful, venal, unprincipled and deeply alluring woman.

Bill turns right into Hall Road and then left into Abbey Road. He's driving fast – the decision to leave the pub had been mutual. He had said, 'It's getting insane in there – looks like they'll be going to a penalty shoot-out. Let's get out of here, go some-where where there's neither sight nor sound of foot-ball, hmm?' And she had said, 'If you like.'

The streets are emptied of traffic – the whole city is inside, watching the match. Bill banks to the right, to the left, he feels the weight of the car shift beneath him like a body. He concentrates on the whine of the transmission and the thrum of the engine. He pokes at the CD and a track with a suitably heavy bass line begins to underscore the tense atmosphere in the car. 'Drive smoothly, avoid fast starts, hard cornering and heavy braking . . .' What the hell do they think anyone wants a Volvo 760 Turbo for, if, as the manual suggests above, it's inadvisable to drive the car with any alacrity?

At Kalmar – where Bill knows from his careful reading of the manual, the Volvo 760 Turbo is built by dedicated teams of workers, rather than by an unconscious and alienated assembly line – they presumably have no need of the car's maximal performance capability. In the sexually tolerant atmosphere of Sweden, the Volvo has evolved as a highly safe vehicle in which to transport the promiscuous. If you're about to start an affair with a fellow worker at the Plant, you simply say to your wife, 'Bibi, I've decided that I must make love to Liv. I shall take the estate today – and a clean duvet!' Whereupon she replies, 'Of course, Ingmar, but remember, "Protective bags should be used to avoid soiling the upholstery" . . .'

'You seem preoccupied?' Bill wouldn't have believed that anyone could actually say this whilst toying with her silken *décolletage* – but Serena just has.

'Mmm . . . s'pose so, work, y'know –'

'Yes! Your work.' Serena stirs her languor into an animated whirl. 'What's it like being a shrink? Have you got any really weird, disturbed patients? D'jew think I'm crazy?'

Bill tilts the car up on to Fitzjohn's Avenue before replying, 'Which of those questions do you want me to answer first?'

'Oh, the last, I suppose . . .'

Christ! The woman knows how to toy – she's a world-class toyer. 'Why on earth do you imagine that you're crazy?'

Serena takes her time answering. She chafes her thighs together so slowly that Bill cannot forbear from imagining the minute accommodations of flesh, hair and membrane that are going on behind the three-buttoned curtain covering her lap. Eventually, when they are level with Lindy's Pâtisserie on Heath Street, she comes back with, 'Bluntly, I find I have to have a really good orgasm every day,' and gives him an amazing smile, her teeth so white and vulpine, her gums so pink.

Bill feels the sweat burst from his armpits like spray from a shower fitment. He grips the wheel so tightly that as the Volvo bucks across the junction with Hampstead High Street, he feels he might wrench it clear off and twist the O of metal, foam and plastic into an involved pretzel shape. Kerrist! He's thinking about adultery in Hampstead – it's gone this far, he keens inside; my life has plunged into a prosaic – prolix even – vanishing point.

At Whitestone Pond they stop in order to allow a man with black-and-white striped trousers to traverse the zebra crossing. Serena doesn't appear to notice this – but Bill does. Bill finds he is noticing every-thing: the golden micro-fleece on the nape of Serena's neck; a model yacht on the pond, tacking neatly around a floating Coke can; to the right of the road the Heath, and beyond it, collapsing waves of concrete and glass and brick and steel – maritime London. 'When you say "a really good orgasm"' – Bill chooses her words carefully – 'do you mean good in a moral sense?'

Serena breaks into trills and even frills of laughter – if that's possible. 'Tee-hee-hee, oh no – not at all! *I* mean a ripping, snorting, tooth-clashing, thor-oughly cathartic orgasm, one that makes me feel as if every individual nerve ending has climaxed. *That* kind of good orgasm.'

'Oh, that kind.' Bill feels certain he's damaged the turbo unit. He habitually does everything to the Volvo's engine that – according to the manual – he shouldn't. He races it immediately after starting, before the cold oil has had a chance to reach all the lubricating points. Worse than that, the engine has also been turned off when the turbo-charger was at high speed – with the risk of seizing or heat damage – although, admittedly it wasn't Bill who'd done it.

It was Vanessa. She managed to lean right across Bill, tear the keys out of the ignition and throw them out the window of the car and clear over the para-pet of the Westway, as the Volvo was ploughing along it at seventy. When they had coasted to a halt, Vanessa threw herself out as well. No one likes to be made a fool of.

Bill parks the car in the small car-park off Hampstead Lane, diagonally opposite to Compton Avenue. They walk out on to the Heath. A light breeze is blowing up here and within seconds it's dried their sweaty brows, cooled their sweaty bodies. They embrace and Bill feels Serena's hair being blown about his chops. It's the closest he's ever been, he realises, to a shampoo commercial.

They walk on, stopping every few yards for more snogging and groping. Bill is certain he has never had a more turgid erection in his life. If he flung himself forward on to the macadamised path, his resilient member would simply bounce him back up again. If he took his trousers off and scampered across the grass he would, to all intents and purposes, be indistinguishable from the famous statuette of Priapus, his penis as large and curved as a bow. Good orgasm, ha! Great orgasm, more like.

On top of Parliament Hill they take their bodies to a bench that faces out over the city, and sit them there to listen to its peculiar silence. From the direction of Gospel Oak a man comes running up the hill. Even from three hundred yards away Bill can see that he's wearing an England football shirt. The man is clearly in some distress; as he nears Bill becomes aware of labouring breath and pumping arms. He comes up to them like someone about to deliver news of a bad naval defeat by the Persians. But instead of collapsing he props himself against their bench saying, 'Iss gone to penalty shoot-outs – I couldn't cope any more.'

He's a small plump man, with a bald pate fringed by a neat horseshoe of grey hair. Clearly football is his life. 'I got meself this fucking big Havana – to celebrate wiv.' He displays the stogie to them, clamped in his humid paw. 'But now I dunno, I dunno, I can't cope –'

'We came here to get away from the football,' says Serena.

'Me too, me too,' the man puffs back.

'Actually' – Bill takes a certain delight in this savage betrayal – 'I bet we'll be able to hear the result from up here.' On cue there's an enormous roar from the city below. 'There we go, that was one goal.'

The three of them wait for two minutes, then there's a second eruption of roaring from the metropolis. They wait another two minutes and . . . nothing. Worse than nothing – a negative roar, a sonic vacuum in which a roar should have been. 'They've missed one . . . the fuckers . . . they've missed one . . .' The little man is destroyed, ripped asunder. He grinds the Havana into the grass with his training shoe, then he heads off back down the hill.

Five minutes later Bill and Serena are rutting in a copse.

4. *Wheel and Tyres*

It is four days later and Bill Bywater sits at the desk which occupies most of the half-landing in his Putney house. Vanessa likes to be by the river; Bill rather wishes she was in it. Bill thinks it suitable that his study should occupy this in-between place, neither up nor down, because he has an in-between kind of psyche – especially at the moment. This is now the terrifyingly tiny house of the urban adulterer and Bill moves about it with incredible subtlety, acutely aware that every movement – from now on and for the rest of his natural life – will constitute a potential, further violation.

Bill sits at the desk and contemplates the Volvo 760 Owner's Manual for the year 1988 – perversely enough the year of his marriage. He has reached the section entitled 'Wheels and Tyres'. Bill smiles manically – he's lost his grip – and reaches for the Tipp-Ex. On the opposing page there's a neat pen-and-wash drawing of a 1957 Volvo Amazon, captioned accordingly. With great deliberation Bill applies the little brush with its clot of liquid paper to the word 'Volvo' and smiles, satisfied by its deletion. It is approximately the hundredth instance of the word that he has dealt with, and soon the manual will become an opaque text, the arcanum of a vanished religion.

As he leafs back through the pages, Bill is deeply satisfied by the small white lozenges of Tipp-Ex smattering them. They look like the results of pin-point accurate ejaculations. Bill, like Freud, has never repudiated or abandoned the importance of sexuality and infantilism, and with this unusual action he is attempting to reorient his sexuality through infantile handiwork. Bill is working hard to convince himself that by eradicating the word 'Volvo' from the manual, he will also annul his obsession with Serena's vulva, which has got quite out of hand.

In the copse she made Bill take off all of his clothes – and all of her own. At last his hands got to go on stage and open her curtain skirt. He shivered despite the summer heat and the close, dusty rot of desiccated shrubbery. 'What's the problem?' she laughed at him, cupping her own breasts, stimulating her own nipples. 'No point in worrying about the cops – we're in it already.' Their clothing made an inadequate stage for the performance that ensued. Bill could never have guessed that such a sexual Socrates would prove so satisfied a pig; she snorted and truffled in the musty compost. They had fucked five times since – top 'n' tailing each other at the top 'n' tail of each day.

Again and again Bill scans the preamble to the section, which admonishes him to 'Read the following pages carefully', but his eyes keep sliding down to the subheading 'Special Rims', what can it mean? On page 67 there are directions for changing wheels, and a photograph of a young woman doing just that. The caption reads: 'Stand next to body.' Bill finds this distracting, but not as much as he does the boldface line further down the page which reads:

'**Make sure that the arm is lodged well in the attachment.**'

Bill sighs and throws down the Tipp-Ex brush. It's no good, it's not working. Instead of the deletion of the word 'Volvo' cancelling out thoughts of Serena's vulva, it's enhancing them. The firm, warm, lubricious embrace of living leather; the smell of saliva and cigarette smoke; the twitter and peep of the CD – a soundtrack for orgasm. Perhaps, Bill thinks, perhaps if I get to the very root of this I'll do better. Perhaps if I delete the word 'Volvo' from the car itself it will do the trick?

Serena has mastered a trick. She can apply ever so slight pressure to Bill's indicator levers and she can effortlessly flick his shift into drive. Serena has undoubtedly read and absorbed the manual. Bill wouldn't be at all surprised to learn that she knew exactly how to grease the nipple on the retractable-type towing bracket. That's the sort of woman she is, as at home in a family car like the Volvo 760, as she would be in a sportier model.

Bill crouches by the radiator grille. The tarmac is so warm on this summer evening that his feet subside a little into the roadway. In his right hand Bill holds a pot of Humbrol metal paint, in his left a brush. He is carefully painting out the word 'Volvo' on the maker's badge of the car. He hears a riffle of rubber wheels and the fluting of a toddler, and turns to see that Vanessa has come up beside him, pushing their son in his buggy.

'Bill' – how can a voice be so cram-packed with wry irony (or 'wiferonry' as Bill awkwardly compounds it – to himself) – 'what on earth are you doing?'

'Whaddya' think?' he snaps.

'I don't know – that's why I asked.' The toddler's eyes are round with anxiety; his life is already characterised by these tonal conflicts between giants, Gog and Magog smiting his Fischer-Price bell.

'I'm getting rid of all the instances of the word "Volvo" on this fucking car – that's what I'm doing.'

'Dada said the F word.' The toddler doesn't lisp – his voice is high and precise.

'Dada wants to rid himself of the F word,' Vanessa pronounces sententiously.

'How true, how true . . .' Bill mutters.

When the buggy and its cargo have disappeared inside the house Bill straightens up; he has arranged to meet Serena in the pub in St John's Wood, and more importantly – he's covered. He holds a seminar at the Middlesex Hospital every Wednesday evening at this time, so Vanessa won't be curious about his absence. Bill stashes the paint and brush in the cardboard box of car impedimenta that he keeps in the boot of the ex-Volvo. He strolls up the path and opening the front door with his key shouts into the crack, 'I'm off!' and at the same time snatches up the CD face-off, his mobile and a sheaf of lecture notes he has to drop off for Sunil Rahman – who is giving the seminar. To Vanessa, who is feeding the toddler in the kitchen, this irruption of sound is just that – an odd kind of effect, as of a train window being opened while passing through a tunnel at speed.

In the ex-Volvo, waiting at the lights by Putney Bridge, Bill dickers with the servos that alter the angle and rake of the driver's seat. One of the servos is on the blink, and if he presses the button too much the seat tilts forward and to the left, threatening to deposit him face down, dangling over the steering wheel, in a posture all too reminiscent of how Bill imagines a suicide would end up after making with a section of hose and watering the interior of the ex-Volvo with exhaust fumes. 'Jesus!' he exclaims out loud as the lights change. 'I've got to stop this!'

Proceeding up Fulham Palace Road Bill faffs around with nodulous buttons until he manages to get Serena's number. He clutches the purring instrument to his ear and hears her recorded pout. When the time comes he leaves a plaint in place of himself: can't make it, lecture, car trouble . . . later. This isn't, of course, the first time that Bill's bailed out of this kind of situation, nor, he suspects, will it be the last.

The lecture notes dropped in reception at the hospital, Bill wheels the big car up on to the Westway and heads out of town. There's only one place for him now, Thame, and only one person he can speak to, Dave Adler, proprietor of the Thame Motor Centre – Repairs and Bodywork Our Speciality. Dave has worked on Bill's Volvo for many years now – ever since he gave up psychiatry. Dave sees no intrinsic design faults in the Volvo 760 Turbo itself, rather he is inclined to locate them in the driver.

Conversations between the two men usually go something like this:

Dr Bill Bywater: Dave? It's Bill.

Dr Dave Adler: Yeah.

Dr BB: There seems to be something wrong with the transmission . . .

Dr DA: Yeah.

Dr BB: The car isn't changing up smoothly, it sort of overrevs and then – well, *surges*.

Dr DA: Have you checked the automatic transmission fluid?

Invariably Bill hasn't checked it, or the windscreen reservoir, or the oil, or the brake fluid, or indeed any of the seething, bubbling liquids that course through the car's blocky body. This will provide Dave Adler with an entrée for a sneer about how ridiculously cavalier Bill is about his car, and how if he would only pay attention to maintenance he wouldn't run into this trouble.

While Bill smiles to himself at the thought of the unscheduled lecture he will receive this evening when he turns up in Thame, the ex-Volvo rumbles down off the flyover and heads west into the soft heart of Britain.

Forty minutes later the car rolls to a halt in a dusty lane that snakes away from the market square of the small Oxfordshire town. The high wooden doors of Dave Adler's garage are shut and chained. Dangling from the hasp of the lock is a peculiar sign which Dave uses in lieu of a more conventional one. The sign reads: 'BEARING IN MIND THE FACT THAT EVERYONE HIDES THE TRUTH IN MATTERS OF SEX – WE'RE CLOSED.' Bill guffaws to himself, albeit a little wearily.

Meanwhile, in Putney, Dave Adler lowers himself carefully into the inspection pit of the Bywaters' marital bed. He has the necessary equipment and he's intent on giving Vanessa Bywater's chassis a really thorough servicing. As far as Dave Adler is concerned a car is a means of transport, nothing more and nothing less.

A Story for Europe

'*Wir-wir*,' gurgled Humpy, pushing his little fingers into the bowl of spaghetti Miriam had just cooked for him. He lifted his hands up to his face and stared hard at the colloidal web of pasta and cheese. '*Wir müssen expandieren!*' he pronounced solemnly.

'Yes, darling, they *are* like worms, aren't they,' said the toddler's mother.

Humpy pursed his little lips and looked at her with his discomfiting bright blue eyes. Miriam held the gaze for a moment, willing herself to suffuse her own eyes with tenderness and affection. Blobs of melted cheese fell from Humpy's hands, but he seemed unconcerned. '*Masse!*' he crowed after some seconds.

'*Very* messy,' Miriam replied, hating the testiness that infected her tone. She began dabbing at the plastic tray of his high chair, smearing the blobs of cheese and coiling the strayed strands of spaghetti into edible casts.

Humpy continued staring at the toy he'd made out of his tea.

'*Masse*,' he said again.

'Put it down, Humpy. Put it in the dish – *in the dish!*' Miriam felt the clutch on her control slipping.

Humpy's eyes widened still more – a typical prelude to tears. But he didn't cry, he threw the whole mess on the just-cleaned floor, and as he did so shouted, '*Massenfertigung!*' or some such gibberish.

Miriam burst into tears. Humpy calmly licked his fingers and appeared obscurely satisfied.

When Daniel got back from work an hour later, mother and son were still not reconciled. Humpy had struggled and fought and bitten his way through the rituals of pre-bedtime. Every item of clothing that needed to be removed had had to be pulled off his resisting form; he made Miriam drag him protesting every inch of the ascent to the bathroom; and once in the bath he splashed and kicked so much that her blouse and bra were soaked through. Bathtime ended with both of them naked and steaming.

But Daniel saw none of this. He saw only his blue-eyed handsome boy, with his angelic brown curls framing his adorable, chubby face. He put his bag down by the hall table and gathered Humpy up in his arms. 'Have you been a good boy while Daddy was at the office –'

'You don't have an office!' snapped Miriam, who like Humpy was in terry-towelling, but assumed in her case for reasons of necessity rather than comfort.

'Darling, darling . . . what's the matter?' Carrying the giggling Humpy, whose hands were entwined in his hair, Daniel advanced towards his wife.

'*Darlehen, hartes Darlehen,*' gurgled Humpy, seemingly mimicking his father.

'If you knew what a merry dance he's led me today, you wouldn't be *quite* so affectionate to the little bugger.' Miriam shrank away from Daniel's kiss. She was worried that, if she softened, let down her Humpy-guard at all, she might start to cry again.

Daniel sighed. 'It's just his age. *All* children go through a difficult phase at around two and a half; Humpy's no exception –'

'That may be so. But not all children are so aggressive. Honestly, Daniel, I swear you don't get to see the half of it. It's not as if I don't give him every ounce of love that I have to give; and he flings it back in my face, along with a lot of gibberish!' And with this Miriam did begin to cry, racking sobs which wrenched her narrow shoulders.

Daniel pulled Miriam to him and stroked her hair. Even Humpy seemed distressed by this turn of events. '*Mutter,*' he said wonderingly, '*Mutter,*' and squirmed around in his father's arms, so as to share in the family embrace.

'See,' said Daniel, 'of course he loves his mother. Now you open a bottle of that nice Chablis, and I'll put young Master Humpy down for the night.'

Miriam blinked back her tears. 'I suppose you're right. You take him up then.' She bestowed a glancing kiss on the top of Humpy's head. Father and son disappeared up the stairs. The last thing Miriam heard before they rounded the half-landing was more of Humpy's peculiar baby talk. '*Mutter-Mutter-Muttergesellschaft*' was what it sounded like. Miriam tried hard to hear this as some expression of love towards herself. Tried hard – but couldn't manage it.

Daniel laid Humpy down in his cot. 'Who's a very sleepy boy then?' he asked.

Humpy looked up at him; his blue eyes were still bright, untainted with fatigue. '*Wende!*' said Humpy cheerily. '*Wende-Wende-Wende!*' He drew his knees up to his chest and kicked them out.

'Ye-es, that's right.' Daniel pulled the clutch of covers up over the bunched little boy. 'Wendy *will* be here to look after you in the morning, because it's Mummy's day to go to work, isn't it?' He leant down to kiss his son, marvelling – as ever – at the tight, intense feeling the flesh of his flesh provoked in him. 'Goodnight, little love.' He turned on the nightlight with its slow-moving carousel of leaping bunnies and clicked off the main light. As Daniel went back downstairs he could still hear Humpy gurgling to himself, '*Wende-Wende,*' contentedly.

But there was little content to be had at the Greens' oval scrubbed-pine kitchen table that evening. Miriam Green had stopped crying, but an atmosphere of fraught weepiness prevailed. 'Perhaps I'm too bloody old for this,' she said to Daniel, thumping a steaming casserole down so that flecks of onion, flageolets and juice spilled on to the table. 'I nearly hit him today, Daniel, hit him!'

'You musn't be so hard on yourself, Miriam. He

is a handful – and you know that it's always the mother who gets the worst of it. Listen, as soon as this job is over I'll take some more time off –'

'Daniel, it isn't that that's the problem.'

And it wasn't, for Miriam Green couldn't complain about Daniel. He did far more childcare than most fathers, and certainly more than any father who was trying to get a landscape-gardening business going in the teeth of a recession. Nor was Miriam cut off from the world of work by her motherhood, the way so many women were, isolated then demeaned by their loss of status. She had insisted on continuing with her career as a journalist after Humphrey was born, although she had accepted a jobshare in order to spend two and a half days a week at home. Wendy, the part-time nanny who covered for Miriam during the rest of the week, was, quite simply, a treasure. Intelligent, efficient and as devoted to Humpy as he was to her.

No, when Miriam Green let fly the remark about being 'too old', her husband knew what it was that was really troubling her. It was the same thing that had troubled her throughout her pregnancy. The first trimester may have been freighted with nausea, the second characterised by a kind of skittish sexiness, and the third swelling to something resembling bulgy beatitude, but throughout it all Miriam Green had felt deeply uneasy. She had emphatically declined the amniocentesis offered by her doctor, although at forty-one the hexagonal chips were not quite stacked in her favour.

'I don't believe in tinkering with destiny,' she had told Daniel, who, although he had not said so, thought the more likely reason was that Miriam felt she had tinkered with destiny too much already, and that this would, in a mysterious way, be weighed in the balance against her. Daniel was sensitive to her feelings, and although they talked around the subject, neither of them ever came right out with it and voiced the awful fear that the baby Miriam was carrying might turn out to be *not quite right*.

In the event the birth was a pure joy – and a revelation. Miriam and Daniel had lingered at home for the first five hours of the labour, mindful of all the premature hospital-dashes their friends had made. When they eventually got to the hospital Miriam's cervix was eight centimetres dilated. It was too late for an epidural, or even pethidine. Humphrey was born exactly fifty-one minutes later, as Miriam squatted, bellowing, on what looked to Daniel suspiciously like a school gym mat.

One moment he was watching the sweating, distending bulk of his wife, her face pushed about by pain; the next he was holding a blue-red ball of howling new vitality. Humphrey was perfect in every way. He scored ten out of ten on the first assessment. His features were no more oriental than those of any other new-born Caucasian baby. Daniel held him tight, and uttered muttered prayers to the idea of a god that might have arranged things so perfectly.

The comfortable Victorian house in Muswell Hill

the Greens called home had long since been tricked out with enough baby equipment to cope with sextuplets. The room designated as the young master's had had a mural of a rainforest painted on its walls by an artist friend, complete with myriad examples of biodiversity. The cot was from Heal's, the buggy by Silver Cross. There were no less than three back-up Milton sterilisers.

Daniel had worried that Miriam was becoming obsessive in the weeks preceding the birth, and after they brought Humpy home from the hospital he watched her closely for any signs of creeping depression, but none came. Humphrey thrived, putting on weight like a diminutive boxer preparing for life's title fight. Sometimes Daniel and Miriam worried that they doted on him too much, but mostly they both felt glad that they had waited to become parents, and that their experience and maturity was part of the reason their child seemed so pacific. He hardly ever cried, or was colicky. He even cut his first two teeth without any fuss. He was, Daniel pronounced, tossing Humpy up in the air while they all giggled, 'a mensch'.

Daniel and Miriam delighted in each stage of Humpy's development. Daniel took roll after roll of out-of-focus shots of his blue-eyed boy, and Miriam pasted them into scrapbooks, then drew elaborate decorative borders around them. Humpy's first backwards crawl, frontwards crawl, trembling step, unassisted bowel movement, all had their memento. But then, at around two, their son's smooth and steady path of development appeared to waver.

Humpy's giggles and gurgles had always been expressive. He was an infant ready to smile, and readier still to give voice. But at that time, when from many many readings of the relevant literature his parents knew he should be beginning to form recognisable words, starting to iterate correctly, Humpy changed. He still gave voice, but the 'Da-das' and 'Ma-mas' garbled in his little mouth; and were then augmented with more guttural gibberish.

Their friends didn't really seem to notice. As far as they were concerned it was just a toddler's rambunctious burbling, but both Daniel and Miriam grew worried. Miriam took Humpy to the family doctor, and then at her instigation to a specialist. Was there some hidden cleft in Humpy's palate? No, said the specialist, who examined Humpy thoroughly and soothingly. Everything was all right inside Humpy's mouth and larynx. Mrs Green really shouldn't be too anxious. Children develop in many diverse ways; if anything – and this wasn't the specialist's particular expertise, he was not a child psychologist – Humpy's scrambled take on the business of language acquisition was probably a sign of an exceptional growing intellect.

Still, relations between mother and son did deteriorate. Miriam told Daniel that she felt Humpy was becoming strange to her. She found his tantrums increasingly hard to deal with. She asked Daniel again and again, 'Is it me? Is it that I'm not relating to him properly?' And again and again Daniel reassured her that it was 'just a stage'.

Sometimes, pushing Humpy around the Quadrant, on her way to the shops on Fortis Green Road, Miriam would pause and look out over the suburban sprawl of North London. In her alienation from her own child, the city of her birth was, she felt, becoming a foreign land. The barely buried anxieties about her age, and how this might be a factor in what was happening to Humpy, clawed their way through the sub-soil of her psyche.

Herr Doktor Martin Zweijärig, Deputy Director of the Venture Capital Research Department of Deutsche Bank, stood at the window of his office on the twentieth storey of the Bank's headquarters building looking out over the jumbled horizon of Frankfurt. All about him, the other concrete peaks of 'Mainhattan', the business and banking district, rose up to the lowering sky. Zweijärig's office window flowed around a corner of the Bank's building, and this, together with his elevated perspective, afforded him a view of the city cut up into vertical slices by the surrounding office blocks.

To his left, he could view an oblong of the university, and beyond it the suburb of Bockenheim; to his right the gleaming steel trapezoid of the Citibank building bisected the roof of the main station, and beyond it the old district of Sachsenhausen. Zweijärig couldn't see the River Main – but he knew it was there. And straight in front of him the massive eminence of the Messeturm, the highest office building in Europe, blotted out most of the town centre, including, thankfully, the mangled modernism of the Zweil shopping centre. Zweijärig had once, idly, calculated that, if a straight line were projected from his office window, down past the right-hand flank of the Messeturm at the level of the fifteenth storey, it should meet the earth two thousand and fifty-seven metres further on, right in the middle of the Goethehaus on Hirschgrab Strasse; forming a twanging, invisible chord, connecting past and present, and perhaps future.

'We must expand!' The phrase with its crude message of commercial triumphalism kept running through Zweijärig's mind, exhorting his inner ear. Why did Kleist feel the need to state the obvious in quite so noisy a fashion? And so early in the morning? Zweijärig didn't resent Kleist's elevation above him in the hierarchy of the Venture Capital Division – it made sense. He was, after all, at fifty-five six years Zweijärig's junior; and even though they had both been with the Bank the same number of years, it was Kleist who had the urge, the drive, to push for expansion, to grapple with the elephantine bureaucracy the Treuhand had become and seek out new businesses in the East for the Bank to take an interest in.

But the rescheduling of the directors' meeting for 7.30 a.m., and the trotting-out of such tawdry pabulums! Why, this morning Kleist had even had the temerity to talk of mass marketing as the logical goal of the Division. 'The provision of seed capital, hard loans even, for what – on the surface – may appear to be ossified, redundant concerns, can be approached at a mass level. We need to get the information concerning the services we offer to the widest possible sector of the business community. If this entails a kind of mass marketing then so be it.'

Zweijärig sighed deeply. A dapper man, of medium height, with a dark, sensual face, he was as ever dressed in a formal, sober, three-piece suit. This was one Frau Doktor Zweijärig had bought at the English shop, Barries, on Goethestrasse. Zweijärig liked the cut of English business suits, and also their conservatism. Perhaps it was because he wasn't a native Frankfurter, but rather a displaced Sudetenlander, that Zweijärig felt the brashness of his adoptive city so keenly. He sighed again, and pushed his spectacles up on his forehead, so that steel rims became enmeshed in wire-wool hair. With thumb and forefinger he massaged his eyes.

He felt airy today, insubstantial. Normally the detail of his work was so readily graspable that it provided his mind with more than enough traction, adhesion to the world. But for the past few days he had felt his will skittering about like a puck on an ice rink. He couldn't seem to hold on to any given thought for more than a few seconds.

Maybe it was a bug of some kind? His daughter, Astrid, had called the previous evening from Stuttgart and said that she definitely had a viral infection. She'd stayed with them at the weekend – perhaps that was it? Zweijärig couldn't remember feeling quite so unenthusiastic about work on a Tuesday morning. Or was it that Kleist's appointment had irked him more than he realised. Right now he would have rather been in the Kleinmarkthalle, buying sausage or pig's ears from Schreiber's; or else at home with Gertrud, pruning the roses on the lower terrace. He conjured up a vision of their house, its wooden walls and wide glass windows merging with the surrounding woodland. It was only twenty kilometres outside Frankfurt, on the north bank of the river, but a world away.

Zweijärig fondled the heavy fob of his car keys in the pocket of his trousers. He pushed the little nipple that opened the central locking on the Mercedes, imagining the car springing into life, rear lights flashing. He pictured it, under autopilot, backing, filling, then driving up from the underground car-park to sit by the kerb in front of the building, waiting to take him home.

'Childish,' he muttered aloud, 'bloody childish.'

'Herr Doktor?' said Frau Schelling, Zweijärig's secretary, who he hadn't realised had entered the room. 'Did you say something?'

'Nothing – it's nothing, Frau Schelling.' He summoned himself, turned from the window to confront her. 'Are those the files on Unterweig?'

'Yes, Herr Doktor. Would you like to go over them

with me now?' Zweijärig thought he detected a note of exaggerated concern in her voice, caught up in the bucolic folds of her Swabian accent.

'No, no, that's all right. As long as the details of the parent company are there as well –'

'Herr Doktor, I'm sorry to interrupt, but Unterweig has no parent company, if you recall. It was only properly incorporated in May of last year.'

'Incorporated? Oh yes, of course, how foolish of me. Please, Frau Schelling, I'm feeling a little faint. You wouldn't mind terribly getting me a glass of water from the cooler?'

'Of course not, Herr Doktor, of course not.'

She put the folder down on the desk and hustled out of the room. Really, thought Zweijärig, I must pull myself together – such weakness in front of Frau Schelling. He pulled out the heavy leather chair, the one he had inhabited for the past sixteen years, brought with him from the posting in Munich. He allowed the smell and feel of the thing to absorb him. He picked up the folders and tamped them into a neat oblong, then laid them down again, opened the cover of the first and began to read:

Unterweig is a metal-working shop specialising in the manufacture of basic steel structures for children's playground equipment. The main plant is situated on the outskirts of Potsdam, and there is an office complex in the north-central district. As ever in these cases it is difficult to reach an effective calculation of capitalisation or turnover. Since May 1992, the shop has managed to achieve incorporation despite a 78 per cent fall in orders . . .

The words swam in front of Zweijärig's eyes. Why bother, he thought. I've read so many reports like this, considered so many investment opportunities, what can this one possibly have to offer that any of the others didn't? And why is it that we persist in this way with the Easterners? He grimaced, remembering that he himself had once been like the Easterners – no, not like them, worse off than them. There had been no one-to-one conversion rate for the little that the Russians had allowed him to take.

A thirteen-year-old boy carrying a canvas bag with some bread in it, a pair of socks and two books. One, the poems of Hölderlin, the other a textbook on calculus, with most of the pages loose in the binding. He could barely remember the long walk into exile any more. It seemed to belong to someone else's past, it was too lurid, too nasty, too brutal, too sad for the man he'd become. Flies gathering on a dead woman's tongue.

Had the fields really been that beautiful in Bohemia? He seemed to remember them that way. Smaller fields than those in the West, softer, and fringed by cherry trees always in bloom. It can't have been so. The cherry trees could only have blossomed for a couple of weeks each year, and yet that's what had stayed with him: the clutches of petals pushed and then burst by the wind, creating a warm, fragrant snowfall. He couldn't face meeting with Bocklin and Schiele at the Frankfurter Hof. He'd rather have a few glasses of stuff somewhere, loosen this damn tie . . . Zweijärig's hand went to his neck without him noticing, and shaking fingers tugged at the knot.

On her way back from the water-cooler Frau Schelling saw her boss's face half-framed by one of the glass panels siding his office. He looked, she thought, old, very old for a man of sixty-one. And in the past few days he seemed unable to concentrate on anything much. Herr Doktor Zweijärig, who was always the very epitome of correctness, of efficiency. She wondered whether he might have suffered a minor stroke. She had heard of such things happening – and the person concerned not even noticing, not even *being able* to notice; the part of the brain that should be doing such noticing suffused with blood. It would be uncomfortable for Frau Schelling to call Frau Doktor Zweijärig and voice her anxieties – but worse if she did nothing. She entered the office quietly and placed the glass of water by his elbow, then silently footed out.

Miriam placed the feeding cup by Humpy's cot and paused for a moment looking down at him. It was such a cliché to say that children looked angelic when they slept, and in Humpy's case it was metaphoric understatement. Humpy appeared angelic when awake; asleep he was like a cherry blossom lodged in the empyrean, a fragment of the divinity. Miriam sighed heavily and clawed a hank of her dark corkscrew curls back from her brow. She'd brought the feeding cup full of apple juice in to forestall Humpy calling for her immediately on awaking. He could get out of his cot easily enough by himself, but she knew he wouldn't until he'd finished the juice.

Miriam silently footed out of Humpy's room. She just needed five more minutes to herself, to summon herself. It had been an agonised night on Humpy's account. Not that he'd kept Miriam and Daniel up personally – he never did that – but it had been a night of reckoning, of debating and of finally deciding that they should keep the appointment with the child psychologist that Dr Peppard had made for them for the following day.

Daniel had gone off to work just after dawn, giving the half-asleep Miriam a snuffly kiss on the back of her neck. 'I'll meet you at the clinic,' he said.

'You be there,' Miriam grunted in reply.

Dr Peppard had shared their misgivings about consulting the child psychologist, their worries that, even at two and a half, Humpy might apprehend the institutional atmosphere of the clinic and feel stigmatised, pathologised, mysteriously different to other toddlers. But more than that, she worried that the Greens were losing their grip on reality; she had seldom seen a happier, better-adjusted child than Humpy. Dr Peppard had great confidence in Philip Weston – he was as good at divining adult malaises as he was those of children. If anyone could help the

Greens to deal with their overweening affection for their child – which Dr Peppard thought privately was the beginning of an extreme, hot-housing tendency – then it would be Philip Weston.

Miriam now lay, face crushed into pillow, one ear registering the *Today Programme* – John Humphrys withering at some junior commissioner in Brussels – the other cocked for Humpy's awakening, his juice-slurping, his agglutinative wake-Miriam-up call.

This came soon enough. '*Bemess-bemess-bemess –!*' he cried, shaking the side of his cot so that it squeaked and creaked. '*Bemessungsgrundlage,*' he garbled.

'All right, Humpy,' Miriam called out to him. 'All right, Humpy love, I'm coming!' then buried her head still further in the pillow. But she couldn't shut it out: '*Bemess-bemess-bemessungsgrundlage!*' Better to get up and deal with him.

An hour or so later Miriam was sitting at her dressing table, which was set in the bay window of the master bedroom, with Humpy on her lap. It was a beautiful morning in late spring and the Greens' garden – which Daniel lavished all of his professional skills on – was an artfully disordered riot of verdancy. Miriam sighed, pulling the squirming Humpy to her breast. Life could be so sweet, so good; perhaps Dr Peppard was right and she was needlessly anxious about Humpy. 'I *do* love you so much, Humpy – you're my favourite boy.' She kissed the soft bunch of curls atop his sweet head.

Humpy struggled in her embrace and reached

out to one of the bottles on the dressing table. Miriam picked it up and pressed it into his fat little palm. 'This is kohl, Humpy – can you say that, "kohl"? Try to.'

Humpy looked at the vial of make-up intently; his small frame felt tense in Miriam's arms. *'Kohl,'* he said. *'Kohl!'* he reiterated with more emphasis.

Miriam broke into peals of laughter. 'That's a clever Humpy!' She stood up, feeling the curious coiled heft of the child as she pulled him up with her. She waltzed Humpy a few steps around the room.

'Kohl!' he cried out merrily, and mother and son giggled and whirled; and would have gone on giggling and whirling were it not for the sound of the front door bell.

'Bugger!' said Miriam, stopping the dance. 'That'll be the postman, we'd better go and see what he wants.'

The change in Humpy was instantaneous – almost frighteningly so. *'Pohl!'* he squealed. *'Pohl-Pohl-Pohl!'* and then all his limbs flew out, his foot catching Miriam in her lower abdomen.

She nearly dropped him. The moment before, the moment of apparently mutual comprehension was gone, and in its place was a grizzling gulf. 'Oh Humpy – please, Humpy!' Miriam struggled to control his flailing arms. 'It's OK, it's OK,' she soothed him, but really it was she who needed the soothing.

Philip Weston entered the waiting room of the Gruton Child Guidance Clinic moving silently on the balls of his feet. He was a large, adipose man, who wore baggy corduroy trousers to disguise his thick legs and bulky arse. Like many very big men he had an air of stillness and poise about him. His moon face was cratered with jolly dimples, and his bright-orange hair stood up in a cartoon flammable ruff. He was an extremely competent clinician, with an ability to build a rapport with even the most disturbed children.

The scene that met his forensically attuned eyes was pacific. The Green family were relaxed in the bright sunny waiting room. Miriam sat leafing through a magazine, Daniel sat by her, working away at the occupational dirt beneath his nails, using the marline-spike on his clasp knife. At their feet was Humpy. Humpy had, with Daniel's assistance, in the fifteen minutes since they'd arrived at the clinic, managed to build a fairly extensive network of Brio toy-train tracks, incorporating a swing bridge and a level crossing. Of his own accord he had also connected up a train, some fifteen cars long, and this he was pushing along with great finesse, making the appropriate 'Woo-woo' noises.

'I'm Philip Weston,' said the child psychologist. 'You must be Miriam and Daniel, and this is –?'

'Humpy – I mean Humphrey.' Miriam Green lurched to her feet, edgy at once.

'Please.' Philip damped her down, and knelt down himself by the little boy. 'Hello, Humpy, how are you today?'

Humpy left off mass-transportation activities and

looked quizzically at the clownish man, his sharp blue eyes meeting Philip's waterier gaze. '*Besser*,' he said at length.

'Better?' queried Philip, mystified.

'*Besser*,' Humpy said again, with solemn emphasis. '*Besserwessi!*' and as if this gobbledygook settled the matter, he turned back to the Brio.

Philip Weston regained the foundation of his big legs. 'Shall we go in,' he said to the Greens, and indicated the open door of his consulting room.

Neither Miriam nor Daniel had had any idea of what to expect from this encounter, but in the event they were utterly charmed by Philip Weston. His consulting room was more in the manner of a bright, jolly nursery, a logical extension of the waiting room outside. While Humpy toddled about, picking up toys from plastic crates, or pulling down picture books from the shelves, the child psychologist chatted with his parents. So engaging and informal was his manner that neither Miriam nor Daniel felt they were being interviewed or assessed in any way – although that was, in fact, what was happening.

Philip Weston chatted their worries out of them. His manner was so relaxed, his demeanour so unjudgmental, that they both felt able to voice their most chilling fears. Was Humpy perhaps autistic? Or brain-damaged? Was Miriam's age in some way responsible for his learning difficulty? To all of these Philip Weston was able to provide instant and total refutation. 'You can certainly set yourselves at rest as far as any autism is concerned,' he told them. 'Humpy engages emotionally and sympathetically with the external world; as you can see now, he's using that stuffed toy to effect a personation. No autistic child ever engages in such role-playing activity.'

Nor, according to Philip, was Humpy in any way retarded: 'He's using two or more coloured pencils in that drawing, and he's already forming recognisable shapes. I think I can tell you with some authority that, if anything, this represents advanced, rather than retarded, ability for a child of his age. If there is a real problem here, Mr and Mrs Green, I suspect it may be to do with a gift rather than a deficiency.'

After twenty minutes or so of chatting and quietly observing Humpy, who continued to make use of Philip Weston's superb collection of toys and diversions, the child psychologist turned his attention directly to him. He picked up a small tray full of outsized marbles from his desk and called to the toddler, 'Humpy, come and look at these.' Humpy came jogging across the room, smiling broadly. In his cute, Osh-Kosh bib 'n' braces, his brown curls framing his chubby face, he looked a picture of health and radiance.

Philip Weston selected one of the marbles and gave it to Humpy. 'Now, Humpy,' he said, 'if I give you two of these marbles' – he rattled the tray – 'will you give me that marble back?' Without even needing to give this exchange any thought Humpy thrust the first marble in the child psychologist's face. Philip took it, put it in the tray, selected two other shiny marbles and gave them to him. Humpy grinned broadly. Philip turned to Miriam and Daniel saying, 'This is really quite exceptional comprehension for a child Humpy's age –' He turned back to Humpy.

'Now, Humpy, if I give you two of these remaining marbles, will you give me those two marbles back?'

Humpy stared at Philip for some seconds, while storm clouds gathered in his blue, blue eyes. The little boy's brow furrowed, and his fist closed tightly around his two marbles. '*Besserwessi!*' he spat at Philip, and then, '*Grundgesetz!*'

It was to Philip's credit, and a fantastic exemplar of his clinical skills, that he didn't react at all adversely to these bits of high-pitched nonsense, but merely put the question again: 'These two marbles, Humpy, for your two, what do you say?'

Humpy opened his hand and looked at the two blue marbles he had in his possession. Philip selected two equally shiny blue marbles from the tray and proffered them. There was silence for some moments while the two parties eyed one another's merchandise. Then Humpy summoned himself. He put one marble very carefully in the side pocket of his overalls, and the other in the bib pocket. This accomplished, he said to Philip with great seriousness, '*Finanzausgleichgesetz,*' turned neatly on his heels, and went back to the scribbling he'd been doing before the child psychologist called him over.

Daniel Green sighed heavily, and passed a hand

through his hair. 'Well, now you've seen it, Philip –
that's the Humpy we deal with most of the time. He
talks this . . . this . . . I know I shouldn't say it, but
it's gibberish, isn't it?'

'Hmmm . . .' Philip was clearly giving the matter
some thought before replying. 'We-ell, I agree, it
doesn't sound like anything recognisably meaningful,
but there is definitely something going on here,
Humpy is communicating *something*, something that
he thinks we might comprehend. There's great deliberation in what he's saying . . . I don't know, I don't
know . . .' He shook his head.

'What?' Miriam was sitting forward on the edge
of her chair; she was trying to remain calm, but her
troubled expression betrayed her. 'What do you
think? Please, don't hold anything back from us.'

'It could be pure speculation. It's something I've
never seen before. I tell you, if I didn't know any
better I'd be prepared to hazard the idea that young
Humpy was originating some kind of idiolect, you
know, a private language. His cognitive skills are, as
I said, quite remarkably developed for his age. If you
don't mind, I'd like to get a second opinion here.'

'What would that entail?' asked Miriam. She was
clearly appalled by this turn of events, but Daniel, by
contrast, was leaning forward, engaged, intrigued.

'Well, it just so happens that we have a Dr
Grauerholtz visiting us here at the Gruton at the
moment. This is a marvellous opportunity. He's a
former director of the clinic, now based at the

Bettelheim Institute in Chicago, *and* he's without doubt the foremost expert on human-language acquisition in either Europe or the USA. If he's available I'd like him to pop in right away and have a chat with Humpy as well. See if we can get to the bottom of this young man's verbal antics. What do you say?'

'What is the basis of assessment?'

'The same as it's always been.'

'Meaning . . . ?'

'Meaning that they did have an open order book, that they did have a capital fund – of some sort. Meaning that both have been subject to the one-on-one conversion rate, and those monies remain in escrow. Meaning that precisely, Herr Doktor.'

'Yes, yes, of course, I know all of that. I know all of that.'

It was late in the morning and Zweijärig was feeling no better – perhaps worse. He'd groped his way through the Unterweig file and now was attempting to discuss its contents with Hassell, his capitalisation expert. At least he'd taken the leap and got Frau Schelling to cancel the meeting with Bocklin and Schiele. 'The unheard-of must be spoken.'

'I'm sorry, Herr Doktor?' Hassell was looking curiously at his boss. Zweijärig noted, inconsequentially, how pink Hassell's forehead was. Pink fading to white at the hairline, just like a slice of ham.

'Ah, um, well . . .' I spoke aloud? Zweijärig fumbled the ball of thought. What is this – am I really losing my marbles? 'I mean to say, the conversion rate, Hassell, it remains as stupid today as when Kohl proposed it. It's wrecked our chances of building the economy the way we might wish to. It doesn't reflect the constitution – such as it was; and it doesn't accord with the law governing redistribution of fiscal apportionments to the Länder.'

Hassell was staring hard at Zweijärig during this speech. It was about the closest he could remember his boss getting to discussing politics directly in the four years they'd worked together. He normally skated around such topics, avoiding them with something approaching flippancy. Hassell steepled his plump fingers on the edge of the desk, pursed his plump lips, and ventured a query. 'So, Herr Doktor, would you have favoured Pohl's proposal? Do you think things would have gone that much smoother?'

'Pohl-Kohl. Kohl-Pohl. It hardly matters which bloody joker we have sitting on top of the Reichstag. We're a nation of displaced people, Herr Hassell. We're displaced from our past, we're displaced from our land, we're displaced from each other. That's the European ideal for you, eh – we're closer to people in Marseilles or Manchester than we are to those in Magdeburg. It's an ideal of mass society rather than homeland, ach!'

Zweijärig was, Hassell noted, breathing heavily, panting almost. His tie was loosened, the top button of his shirt undone. Hassell didn't wish to be intrusive, but he ought really to enquire. 'Are you feeling all right, Herr Doktor?'

'All right, yes, yes, Herr Hassell, I feel all right. I feel like the smart-aleck Westerner I've become, eh? Wouldn't you say?'

'It's not my position, Herr Doktor –'

'No, no, of course not, of course not. It's not your position. I'm sorry, Herr Hassell, I'm not myself today, I'm like Job on his dungheap – you know that one, d'you? It's in the Stadel, you should go and look at it. *Job on his Dungheap*. Except in *our* case the dungheap is built of glass and steel, hmm?'

'Dungheap, Herr Doktor?' said Hassell, trying to look unobtrusively over his shoulder, trying to see whether Frau Schelling was in the outer office.

'Playing with shit, Herr Hassell, playing with shit. Have you ever heard the expression that money *is* shit, Herr Hassell?'

'Herr Doktor?'

'Money *is* shit. No, well, I suppose not. Y'know, there are ghosts here in Frankfurt, Herr Hassell, you can see them if you squint. You can see them walking about – the ghosts of the past. This city is built on money, so they say. Perhaps it's built on shit too, hmm?'

And with this gnomic – if not crazy – remark, Herr Doktor Martin Zweijärig stood up, passed a sweaty hand across his brow, and made for the door of his office, calling over his shoulder, 'I'm going for a glass of stuff, Herr Hassell. If you would be so good, please tell Frau Schelling I'll be back in a couple of hours.' Then he was gone.

Hassell sighed heavily. The old man was unwell, disturbed even. He was clearly disoriented; perhaps Hassell should stop him leaving the bank building? Ethics and propriety did battle in the arid processes of Hassell's mind for some seconds, until ethics won – narrowly.

Hassell got up and quit the office at a near-jog, the bunches of fat above his broad hips jigging like panniers on a donkey. But when he reached the lifts Zweijärig had gone. He turned back to the office and met Frau Schelling. 'The Deputy Direktor, Frau Schelling, do you think –?'

'I think he's ill, Herr Hassell – he's behaving very oddly. I called Frau Doktor Zweijärig just now. I hated going behind his back like that, but –'

'You did the right thing, Frau Schelling. What did Frau Doktor Zweijärig say?'

'Oh, she's noticed it as well. She's driving into town right now. She says she'll be here within the hour. But where has he gone?'

'He said something about getting a glass of stuff. Do you think he's gone to Sachsenhausen?'

'I doubt it, he can't stand the GIs there. No, there's a tavern near the station he often goes to. I'll bet he's gone there now.' Frau Schelling shook her head sorrowfully. 'Poor man, I do hope he's all right.'

'Miriam and Daniel Green, this is Dr Grauerholtz . . . and this is Humpy.' Philip Weston stood in the middle of his consulting room making the introductions. Dr

Grauerholtz was a tiny little egg of a man, bald, bifo-
caled, and wearing a quite electric suit. The contrast
between the two psychologists was straightforwardly
comic, and despite the seriousness of the situation,
Daniel and Miriam exchanged surreptitious grins and
jointly raised their eyebrows.

'Hello,' said Dr Grauerholtz warmly. He had a
thick but not unpleasant German accent. 'Philip tells
me that we have a most unusual young fellow with
us today – you must be very proud of him.'

'Proud?' Miriam Green was becoming agitated
again. Dr Grauerholtz and Philip Weston exchanged
meaningful glances. Dr Grauerholtz indicated that
they should all sit down. Then, with rapid, jerky
movements he stripped off his funny jacket, threw it
over a chair, reversed the chair, and sat down on it
facing them with his elbows crossed on the back.

'I don't think I will be in any way upsetting you,
Mr and Mrs Green, if I tell you that my colleague
has managed to do a rudimentary Stanford-Binet test
on Master Humpy –'

'Stanford-Binet?' Miriam was becoming queru-
lous.

'I'm sorry, so-called intelligence test. Obviously
such things are very speculative with such a young
child, but we suspect that Humpy's IQ may be well
up in the hundred and sixties. He is, we believe, an
exceptionally bright young fellow. Now, if you don't
mind . . .'

Dr Grauerholtz dropped backwards off the chair

on to his knees and then crawled towards Humpy across the expanse of carpet. Humpy, who had paid no attention to Dr Grauerholtz's arrival, was playing with some building blocks in the corner of the room. He had managed to construct a sort of pyramid, or ziggurat, the top of which was level with the first shelf of a bookcase, and now he was running toy cars up the side of this edifice and parking them neatly by the spines of the books.

'That's a good castle you've got there, Humpy,' said Dr Grauerholtz. 'Do you like castles?'

Humpy stopped what he was doing and regarded the semi-recumbent world authority on human-language acquisition with an expression that would have been called contemptuous in an older individual. '*Grundausbildung!*' he piped, scooting one of the toy cars along the shelf. Dr Grauerholtz appeared rather taken aback, and sat back on his heels. Daniel and Miriam gave each other weary looks.

'*Grundausbildung?*' Dr Grauerholtz repeated the gibberish with an interrogative-sounding swoop at the end. Humpy stopped what he was doing, tensed, and turned to give the doctor his full attention. '*Ja,*' he said after a few moments, '*grundausbildung.*'

'*Grundausbildung für . . . ?*' gargled the doctor.

'*Für bankkreise,*' Humpy replied, and smiled broadly.

The doctor scratched the few remaining hairs on his head, before saying, 'Humpy, *verstehen sie Deutsch?*'

'*Ja,*' Humpy came back, and giggled. '*Geschäft*

Deutsch.' Then he resumed playing with the toy car, as if none of this bizarre exchange were of any account.

Dr Grauerholtz stood up and came back to where the adults were sitting. They were all staring at him with frank astonishment, none more so than Miriam Green. To look at her you might have thought she was in the presence of some prophet, or messiah. 'Doc-Doctor Grau-Grauerholtz,' she stuttered, 'c-can you understand what Humpy is saying?'

'Oh yes,' the Doctor replied. He was now grinning as widely as Humpy. 'Quite well, I think. You see, your son is speaking . . . How can I put it? He's speaking what you would call "business German".'

'"Business German"?' queried Philip Weston. 'Isn't that a bit unusual for an English child of two and a half?'

Dr Grauerholtz had taken his bifocals off and was cleaning them with a small soft cloth that he'd taken from his trouser pocket. He looked at the three faces that gawped at him with watery, myopic eyes, and then said, 'Yes, yes, I suppose a bit unusual, but hardly a handicap.' He smiled, a small wry smile. 'Some people might say it was a great asset – especially in today's European situation, yes?'

Humpy chose that moment to push over the pyramid of building blocks he'd made. They fell with a delightful local crash; and Humpy began to laugh. It was the happy, secure laugh of a well-loved child – if a tad on the guttural side.

★

They found Herr Doktor Martin Zweijärig sitting on the pavement outside the station. His suit was scuffed-about and dirty, his face was sweaty and contorted. All around him the human flotsam streamed: Turkish guest workers, junkies, asylum-seekers and tourists. There was hardly an ethnic German to be found in this seedy quarter of the European financial capital. Zweijärig was conscious, but barely so. The stroke had robbed him of his strength – he was as weak as a two-year-old child; and quite naturally – he was talking gibberish.

POCKET PENGUINS